"Anthony Horowitz is the lion of children's
literature." Michael Morpurgo

"Horowitz has become a writer who
converts boys to reading."
The Times

"A first-class children's novelist."
TES

Other Diamond Brothers books
The Falcon's Malteser
Public Enemy Number Two
South By South East
The Blurred Man
I Know What You Did Last Wednesday

The Alex Rider™ books
Stormbreaker
Point Blanc
Skeleton Key
Eagle Strike
Scorpia
Ark Angel

The Power of Five™ series
Raven's Gate
Evil Star
Nightrise

Other books by the same author
The Devil and His Boy
Granny
Groosham Grange
Return to Groosham Grange
The Switch

THE FRENCH CONFECTION

ANTHONY HOROWITZ

**WALKER
BOOKS**

First published 2002 by Walker Books Ltd
87 Vauxhall Walk, London SE11 5HJ

This edition published 2007

2 4 6 8 10 9 7 5 3 1

Text © 2002 Anthony Horowitz
Cover illustration © 2007 Martin Chatterton

This book has been typeset in Sabon

Printed in Great Britain by Cox & Wyman Ltd, Reading, Berkshire

British Library Cataloguing in Publication Data:
a catalogue record for this book is available
from the British Library

ISBN 978-1-4063-0492-3

www.walkerbooks.co.uk

CONTENTS

THE FRENCH FOR MURDER

Everybody loves Paris. There's an old guy who even wrote a song about it. "I love Paris in the springtime…", that's how it goes. Well, all I can say is, he obviously never went there with my big brother, Tim. I did – and it almost killed me.

It all started with a strawberry yoghurt.

It was a French strawberry yoghurt, of course, and it was all we had in the fridge for breakfast. Tim and I tossed a coin to decide who'd get the first mouthful. Then we tossed the coin to see who'd keep the coin. Tim won both times. So there I was sitting at the breakfast table chewing my nails, which was all I had to chew, when Tim suddenly let out a great gurgle and started waving his spoon in the air like he was trying to swat a fly.

"What is it, Tim?" I asked. "Don't tell me! You've found a strawberry!"

"No, Nick! Look…!"

He was holding up the silver foil that he'd just torn off the yoghurt carton and looking at it, and now I understood. The company that made the yoghurt was having one of those promotions. You've probably seen them on chocolate bars or crisps or Coke cans. These days you can't even open a can of beans without finding out if you've won a car or a holiday in Mexico or a cheque for a thousand pounds. Personally, I'm just grateful if I actually find some beans. Anyway, the yoghurt people were offering a whole range of prizes and there it was, written on the underside of the foil.

Congratulations from Bestlé Fruit Yoghurts! You have just won a weekend for two in Paris! Just telephone the number printed on the carton for further details and … Bon Voyage!

"I've won, Nick!" Tim gasped. "A weekend for two…!" He stopped and bit his thumb. "Who shall I take?" he muttered.

"Oh thanks a lot, Tim," I said. "It was me who bought the yoghurt."

"But it was my money."

"If it hadn't been for me, you'd have spent it on a choc-ice."

Tim scowled. "But Paris, Nick! It's the most romantic city in Europe. I want to take my girlfriend."

"Tim," I reminded him. "You haven't got a girlfriend."

That was a bit cruel of me. The truth was, Tim hadn't been very lucky in love. His first serious relationship had ended tragically when his girlfriend had tried to murder him. After that he'd replied to one of those advertisements in the lonely hearts column of a newspaper, but he can't have read it properly because the girl had turned out to be a guy who spent the evening chasing him round Paddington station. His last girlfriend had been a fire eater in a local circus. He'd taken her out for a romantic, candlelit dinner but she'd completely spoiled it by eating the candles. Right now he was on his own. He sometimes said he felt like a monk – but without the haircut or the religion.

Anyway, we argued a bit more but finally he picked up the telephone and rang the number on the yoghurt carton. There was no answer.

"That's because you've telephoned the sell-by date," I told him. I turned the carton over. "This is the number here..."

And that was how, three weeks later, we found ourselves standing in the forecourt at Waterloo station. Tim was carrying the tickets. I was carrying the bags. It had been more than a year since we'd been abroad – that had been to Amsterdam on the trail of the mysterious assassin known as Charon – and that time we had gone by ferry. Tim had been completely seasick even before he reached the sea. I was relieved that this time we were going by train, taking the Channel Tunnel, although with Tim, of course, you never knew.

We took the escalator down to the international terminal. Ahead of us, the tunnel was waiting: a thirty-two mile stretch linking England and France, built at a cost of twelve billion pounds.

"You have to admit," Tim said. "It's an engineering marvel."

"That's just what I was thinking," I said.

"Yes. It's a fantastic escalator. And so much faster than going down the stairs…"

We had two seats next to each other right in the middle of one of the carriages. The train was pretty full and soon we were joined by two other passengers opposite us. They were both travelling alone. The first was from Texas – you could tell just from his hat. He was chewing an unlit cigar (this was a non-smoking compartment) and reading a magazine: *International Oil*. The other passenger was a very old lady with white hair and skin so wrinkled I was amazed it managed to stay on. I wasn't sure if she had huge eyes or extremely powerful spectacles but every time she looked at me I thought I was about to be hit by a pair of grey and white golf balls. I looked out of the window. The platform was already empty, sweeping in a graceful curve beneath the great glass canopy. Somewhere a door slammed.

The train left exactly on time at ten minutes past ten. There was no whistle. No announcement. I wouldn't have known we had moved if it hadn't been for the slight shudder – and even that was Tim, not the train. He was obviously excited.

About an hour later there was an announcement on the intercom and we dipped into the tunnel carved out underneath the sea. That was a non-event too. A car-park, a sign advertising hamburgers, a white cement wall and suddenly the outside world disappeared to be replaced by rushing blackness. So this was the engineering miracle of the last century? As far as Eurostar was concerned, it was just a hole in the ground.

Tim had been ready with his camera and now he drew back, disappointed. "Is this it?" he demanded.

I looked up from my book. "What were you expecting, Tim?" I asked.

"I thought this train went under water!" Tim sighed. "I wanted to take some pictures of the fish!"

The other passengers had heard this and somehow it broke the silence. The old lady had been knitting what looked like a multi-coloured sack but now she looked up. "I love taking the train," she announced, and for the first time I realized that she was French. Her accent was so thick you could have wrapped yourself in it to keep warm.

"It sure is one hell of a thing," the Texan agreed. "London to Paris in three and a half hours. Great for business."

The Texan held up his magazine. "I'm in oil. Jed Mathis is the name."

"Why do you call your oil Jed Mathis?" Tim asked.

"I'm sorry?" Jed looked confused. He turned to the old lady. "Are you visiting your grandchildren in Paris?" he asked.

"Non!" the lady replied.

Tim dug into his pocket and pulled out a French dictionary. While he was looking up the word, she continued in English.

"I have a little cake shop in Paris. Erica Nice. That's my name. Please, you must try some of my almond slices." And before anyone could stop her, she'd pulled out a bag of cakes which she offererd to us all.

We were still hurtling through the darkness. Tim put away his dictionary and helped himself. At the same time, a steward approached us, pushing one of those trolleys piled up with sandwiches and coffee. He was a thin, pale man with a drooping moustache and slightly sunken eyes. The name on his badge was Marc Chabrol. I remember thinking even then that he looked nervous. A nervous traveller, I

12

thought. But then, why would a nervous traveller work on a train?

Jed produced a wallet full of dollars and offered to buy us all coffee. A free breakfast and we hadn't even arrived. Things were definitely looking up.

"So what do you do?" Erica Nice asked, turning to Tim.

Tim gave a crooked smile. It was meant to make him look smart but in fact he just looked as though he had toothache. "I'm a private detective," he said.

The steward dropped one of the coffee cups. Fortunately, he hadn't added the water yet. Coffee granules showered over the KitKats.

"A private detective?" Erica trilled. "How very unusual!"

"Are you going to Paris on business?" the Texan asked.

Now of course the answer was "no". We were on holiday. Tim hadn't had any business for several weeks and even then he had only been hired to find a missing dog. In fact he had spent three days at Battersea Dogs' Home where he had been bitten three times – twice by dogs. The trouble was, though, he was never going to admit this. He liked to think of himself as a man of mystery. So now he winked and leaned forward. "Just between you and me," he drawled, "I'm on a case." Yes. A nutcase, I thought. But he went on.

"I've been hired by Interplop."

"You mean Interpol," the Texan said.

"The International Police," Tim agreed. "It's a top-secret case. It's so secret, they don't even know about it at the top. In other words..." He gestured with his almond slice, spraying Jed with crumbs, "...a case for Tim Diamond."

The steward had obviously heard all this. As he put down the first cup of coffee, his hands were shaking so much that the liquid spilled over the table. His face had been pale to begin with. Now it had no colour at all. Even his moustache seemed to have faded.

"Where are you staying in Paris?" the old lady asked.

"It's a hotel called The Fat Greek," Tim said.

"Le Chat Gris," I corrected him. It was French for "grey cat" and this was the name of the hotel where Bestlé Yoghurts had booked us in for three nights.

The name seemed to have an electric effect on the steward. I'd been watching him out of the corner of my eye and actually saw him step backwards, colliding with the trolley. The bottles and cans shook. Two packets of gingerbread biscuits rocketed onto the floor. The man was terrified. But why?

"Paris is so beautiful in the spring," the old lady said. She'd obviously seen the effect that

Tim was having on the steward and perhaps she was trying to change the subject before the poor man had a heart attack. "You must make sure you take a stroll on the Champs Elysées … if you have the time."

"How much do I owe you for the coffee?" the American asked.

"Four euros, monsieur…" The steward reached down and picked up the biscuits. The way he took the money and moved off, he could have been trying to get to Paris ahead of the train. I guessed he wanted to get away from us as fast as he could. And I was right. He didn't even stop to offer anyone else in the carriage a coffee. He simply disappeared. Later, when I went to the loo, I saw the trolley standing on its own in the passageway.

Twenty minutes after we'd entered the tunnel, the train burst out again. There was nothing to show that we'd left one country and entered another. The French cows grazing in the fields looked just the same as the English ones on the other side. An official came past, looking at passports. Erica Nice looked at Tim as if puzzled in some way and went back to her knitting. Jed returned to his magazine. We didn't speak for the rest of the journey.

We arrived at the Gare du Nord about an hour later. As everyone struggled with their luggage, Tim gazed at the name. "When do we arrive in Paris?" he asked.

"Tim, this is Paris," I told him. "The Gare du Nord means north station. There are lots of stations in the city."

"I hope you have a lovely time," Erica Nice said. She had an old carpet-bag. It was big enough to hold a carpet – and maybe that was what she had been knitting. She winked at Tim. "Good luck with the case, mon ami!"

Meanwhile, the Texan had grabbed a leather briefcase. He nodded at us briefly and joined the queue for the exit. Tim and I retrieved our two bags and a few moments later we were standing on the platform, wondering which way to go.

"We'd better find the Metro," I said. Bestlé had given us some spending money for the weekend but I didn't think it would be enough for us to travel everywhere by taxi.

Tim shook his head. "Forget the metro, Nick," he said. "Let's take the tube."

I didn't even bother to argue. I knew a little French – I'd been learning it from a little Frenchman who taught at our school – and I knew, for example, that Metro was the French word for tube train. On the other hand, I didn't know the French for idiot, which was the English word for Tim. I picked up the bags and prepared to follow him when suddenly we found ourselves interrupted.

It was Marc Chabrol. The French steward had reappeared and was standing in front of us, blocking our way. He was terrified. I could see it in his bulging eyes, the sweat on his cheeks, the yellow and black bow tie which had climbed halfway up his neck.

"I have to talk to you, Monsieur," he rasped. He was speaking in English, the words as uncomfortable in his mouth as somebody else's false teeth. "Tonight. At eleven o'clock. There is a café in the sixth *arrondisement*. It is called La Palette…"

"That's very nice of you," Tim said. He seemed to think that Chabrol was inviting us out for a drink.

"Beware of the mad American!" The steward whispered the words as if he were too afraid to speak them aloud. "The mad American…!"

He was about to add something but then his face changed again. He seemed to freeze as if his worst nightmare had just come true. I glanced left and right but if there was someone he had recognized in the crowd, I didn't see them. *"Oh mon Dieu!"* he whispered. He seized Tim's hand and pressed something into the palm. Then he turned and staggered away.

Tim opened his hand. He was holding a small blue envelope with a gold star printed on the side. I recognized it at once. It was a sachet of sugar from the train. "What was all that about?" Tim asked.

I took the sugar and examined it. I thought

he might have written something on it – a telephone number or something. But it was just a little bag of sugar. I slipped it into my back pocket. "I don't know…" I said. And I didn't. Why should the steward have left us with a spoonful of sugar? Why did he want to meet us later that night? What was going on?

"Funny people, the French," Tim said.

Ten minutes later, we were still at the Gare du Nord. The money that Bestlé had given us was in English pounds and pence. We needed euros and that meant queuing up at the Bureau de Change. The queue was a long one and it seemed to be moving at a rate of one euro per hour.

We had just reached the window when we heard the scream.

It was like no sound I had ever heard, thin and high and horribly final. The station was huge and noisy but the scream cut through the crowd like a scalpel. Everybody stopped and turned to see where it had come from. Even Tim heard it. "Oh dear," he said. "It sounds like someone has stepped on a cat."

Tim changed thirty pounds, and taking the money we moved in the direction of the Metro. Already a police car had arrived and several uniformed gendarmes were hurrying towards the trains. I strained to hear what the crowd was saying. They were speaking French, of course. That didn't make it any easier.

"What's happened?"

"It's terrible. Somebody has fallen under a train."

"It was a steward. He was on the train from London. He fell off a platform."

"Is he hurt?"

"He's dead. Crushed by a train."

I heard all of it. I understood some of it. I didn't like any of it. A steward? Off the London train? Somehow I didn't need to ask his name.

"Tim," I asked. "What's the French for murder?"

Tim shrugged. "Why do you want to know?"

"I don't know." I stepped onto the escalator and allowed it to carry me down. "I've just got a feeling it's something we're going to need."

LE CHAT GRIS

Le Chat Gris was in the Latin quarter, a dark, busy area on the south side of the River Seine. Here the streets were full of students and the smell of cheap food. It was a small, narrow building, wedged between an art gallery and a café. A metal cat, more rusty than grey, hung over the main entrance and there were brightly coloured flowers in the front windows. On closer inspection they turned out to be made of plastic.

The reception area was so small that if you went in too quickly you'd be out the other side. There was a receptionist standing behind the desk which was just as well as there wasn't enough room for a chair. He was an old man, at least sixty, with a crumpled face and something terribly wrong with his eyes. When he looked at our passports he had to hold them up beside his ear. He took our names, then sent us to a room on the fifth floor. Fortunately there was a lift but it wasn't much bigger than a telephone box. Tim and I stood shoulder to shoulder with our cases as it creaked and trembled slowly up. Next time, I decided, I'd take the stairs.

The truth was that Bestlé hadn't been too generous with the accommodation. Our room was built into the roof with wooden beams that sloped down at strange angles. It made me think of the Hunchback of Notre Dame. You needed a hunched back to avoid hitting your head on the ceiling. There were two beds, a single window with a view over the other rooftops, a chest of drawers and a bathroom too small to take a bath.

"Which bed do you want?" I asked.

"This one!" Tim threw himself onto the bed next to the window. There was a loud "ping" as several of the springs snapped. I sat down, more carefully, on the other bed. It felt like the duvet wasn't just filled with goose feathers, but they'd also left in half the goose.

We dumped our luggage and went out. This was, after all, Thursday morning and we only had until Sunday afternoon. Back in the reception area, the receptionist was talking to a new arrival. This was a square-shouldered man with narrow eyes and black, slicked-back hair. He was wearing an expensive, charcoal grey suit. Both of them stopped when they saw us.

I dropped the key with a clunk.

"*Merci,*" I said.

Neither of the men said anything. Maybe it was my accent.

There was a mirror next to the front door and but for that I wouldn't have noticed what happened next. But as Tim and I made our way out, the man in the grey suit reached out and took my key, turning it round so that he could read the number. He was interested in us. That was for sure. His eyes, empty of emotion, were still scrutinizing us as the door swung shut and we found ourselves in the street.

First the death of the steward on the train. Then the last whispered warning: "*Beware the mad American!*" And now this. There was a nasty smell in the air and already I knew it wasn't just French cheese.

"Which way, Nick?" Tim was waiting for me, holding a camera. He had already taken three photographs of the hotel, a streetlamp and a post-box and he was waiting for me in the morning sunlight. I wondered if he had remembered to put in a film.

I thought for a moment. I was probably being stupid. We were here in Paris for the weekend and nothing was going to happen. I couldn't even be sure that it really was Marc Chabrol who had fallen under the train. "Let's try down there," I said, pointing down the street.

"Good idea," Tim agreed as he turned the other way.

What can I tell you about Paris? I'm no travel writer. I'm not crazy about writing and I can't usually afford to travel. But anyway...

Paris is a big city full of French people. It's a lot prettier than London and for that matter so are the people. They're everywhere: in the street-side cafés, sipping black coffee from thimble-sized cups, strolling along the Seine in their designer sunglasses, snapping at each other on the bridges through eighteen inches of the latest Japanese lens. The streets are narrower than in London and looking at the traffic you get the feeling that war has broken out. There are cars parked everywhere. On the streets and on the pavements. Actually, it's hard to tell which cars are parked and which ones are just stuck in the traffic jams. But the strange thing is that nobody seems to be in a hurry. Life is just a big jumble that moves along at its own pace and if you're in a hurry to leave then maybe you should never have come there in the first place.

That first day, Tim and I did the usual tourist things. We went up the Eiffel Tower. Tim fainted. So we came down again. We went to the cathedral of Notre Dame and I took a picture of Tim and another of a gargoyle. I just hoped that when I got them developed I'd remember which was which. We went up the Champs Elysées and down the Jardin des Tuileries. By lunch-time, my stomach was rumbling. So, more worryingly, were my feet.

We had an early supper at a brasserie overlooking another brasserie. That's another thing about Paris. There are brasseries everywhere. Tim ordered two ham sandwiches, a beer for him and a Coke for me. Then I ordered them again using words the waiter understood. The sandwiches arrived: twenty centimetres of bread, I noticed, but only ten centimetres of ham.

"This is the life, eh, Nick?" Tim sighed as he sipped his beer.

"Yes, Tim," I said. "And this is the bill."

Tim glanced at it and swallowed his beer the wrong way. "Ten euros!" he exclaimed. "That's ... that's...!" He frowned. "How much is that?"

"A euro's worth about seven old francs," I explained. "It's about seventy pence. So the bill is about seven quid."

Tim shook his head. "I hate this new money," he said.

"I know," I agreed. "Because you haven't got any."

We were walking back in the direction of the hotel when it happened. We were in one of those quiet, antique streets near the Seine when two men appeared, blocking our way. The first was in his forties, tall and slim, wearing a white linen suit that was so crumpled and dirty, it hung off him like a used paper bag. He was one of the ugliest men I had ever seen. He had green eyes, a small nose and a mouth like a knife wound. None of these were in quite the right place. It was as if his whole face had been drawn by a six-year-old child.

His partner was about twenty years younger with the body of an ape and, if the dull glimmer in his eyes was anything to go by, a brain to match. He was wearing jeans and a leather jacket and smoking a cigarette. I guessed he was a body-builder. He had muscles bulging everywhere and a neck that somehow managed to be wider than his head. His hair was blonde and greasy. He had fat lips and a tiny beard sprouting out of the middle of his chin.

"Good evening," White Suit said in perfect English. His voice came out like a whisper from a punctured balloon. "My name is Bastille. Jacques Bastille. My friend's name is Lavache. I wonder if I might speak with you."

"If you want to know the way, don't ask us!" Tim replied. "We're lost too."

"I'm not lost. Oh, no." Bastille smiled, revealing teeth the colour of French mustard. "No. But I want to know what he told you. I want to know what you know."

Tim turned to me, puzzled.

"What exactly do you mean?" I asked.

"The steward on the train. What did he tell

you?" There was a pause. Then … "Lavache!"

Bastille nodded and his partner produced what looked like a little model of that famous statue, the Venus de Milo. You know the one. The naked woman with no arms that stands somewhere in the Louvre.

"No thank you," Tim began. "We're not…"

Lavache pressed a button and ten centimetres of razor-sharp metal sprang out of the head of the statue. It was a neat trick. I don't think the real statue ever did that.

Tim stared at it.

"Where is it?" Bastille demanded.

"Your friend's holding it in his hand!" Tim gasped.

"Not the knife! *Sacré bleu!* Are all the English such idiots? I am talking about the object. The item that you were given this morning at the Gare du Nord."

"I wasn't given anything!" Tim wailed.

"It's true," I said, even though I knew that it wasn't.

Bastille blinked heavily. "You're lying."

"No, we're not," Tim replied. "Cross my heart and hope to…"

"Tim!" I interrupted.

"Kill them both!" Bastille snapped.

They really did mean to kill us there and then in that quiet Paris street. Lavache lifted the knife, his stubby fingers curving around the base, a bead of saliva glistening at the corner of his mouth. I glanced back, wondering if we could run. But it was hopeless. We'd be cut down before we could take a step.

"The older one first," Bastille commanded.

"That's him!" Tim said, pointing at me.

"Tim!" I exclaimed.

The knife hovered between us.

But then suddenly a party of American tourists turned the corner – about twenty of them, following a guide who was holding an umbrella with a Stars and Stripes attached to the tip. They were jabbering excitedly as they descended on us. There was nothing Bastille and Lavache could do. Suddenly they were surrounded, and realizing this was our only chance I grabbed hold of Tim and moved away, keeping a wall of American tourists between us and our attackers. Only when we'd come to the top of the street where it joined the wide and busy Boulevard St Michel did we break away and run.

But the two killers weren't going to let us get away quite so easily. I glanced back and saw them pushing their way through the crowd. Bastille shoved out a hand and one of the tourists, an elderly woman, shrieked and fell backwards into a fountain. Several of the other tourists stopped and took photographs of her. Bastille stepped into the road. A car swerved to avoid him and crashed into the front of a restaurant. Two lobsters and a plateful of mussels were sent flying. Someone screamed.

It still wasn't dark. The streets were full of people on their way to restaurants, too wrapped up in their own affairs to notice two English visitors running for their lives. I had no idea where I was going and I wasn't going to stop and ask for directions. I grabbed Tim again and steered him up an alleyway with dozens more restaurants on both sides. A waiter in a long white apron, carrying several trays laden with plates and glasses, stepped out in front of me. There was no way I could avoid him. There was a strangled cry, then a crash.

"Excusez-moi!" Tim burbled.

Fortunately, I didn't know enough French to understand the waiter's reply.

The alleyway brought us back to the Seine. I could see Notre Dame in the distance. Only a few hours before we had been standing on one of its towers, enjoying the view. How could our holiday have become a nightmare so quickly?

"This way, Tim!" I shouted.

I pulled him across a busy street, cars screeching to a halt, horns blaring. A gendarme turned round to face us, a whistle clenched between his teeth, his hands scrabbling for his gun. I swear he would have shot us except that we were already on the other side of the road and a few seconds later Bastille had reached him, brutally pushing him out of the way. The unfortunate gendarme spun round and collided with a cyclist. Both of them collapsed in a tangle of rubber and steel. The last I saw of the gendarme, he had got back to his feet and was shouting at us, making a curious, high-pitched noise. Evidently he had swallowed his whistle which had now got lodged in his throat.

The river was now right in front of us with a pedestrian bridge leading over to the other side. Bastille and Lavache were already crossing the road, blocked for a moment by a bus that had slipped in between them and us.

"The river!" I said.

Tim reached into his pocket and took out his camera.

"No!" I yelled. "I don't want you to photograph it! I want us to cross it!"

We ran onto the bridge, but I hadn't taken more than a few steps before I saw that we'd made a bad mistake. The bridge was closed. There was a tall barrier running across the middle of it with a MEN AT WORK sign – but no sign at all of any men actually at work. They had left their tools, though. There was a wheelbarrow, a pile of steel girders, a cement mixer ... even if we could have climbed over the fence it would have been hard to get through.

"We've got to go back!" I shouted.

But it was too late. Bastille and Lavache had already arrived at the entrance to the bridge and were moving more slowly, both of them smiling. They knew they had us trapped. Lavache had his knife out. It was difficult to hear with the noise of the traffic, but I think he was humming.

We couldn't go back. We couldn't climb the fence. If we jumped over the side, we'd probably drown. This was only March and the water would be ice-cold. Just twenty metres separated us from the two Frenchmen. There was nothing we could do.

And that was when I saw the boat. It was what they called a Bateau Mouche, one of those long, elegant boats with glass windows and ceilings that carry tourists up and down the river throughout the day and night. This one was full of people enjoying a dinner and dance. I heard the music drifting up to us. They were playing a waltz, the "Blue Danube". A strange choice considering they were on the Seine. Already the boat was slipping under the bridge. Another few seconds and it would have disappeared down towards the Eiffel Tower.

"Jump, Tim!" I ordered.

"Right, Nick!" Tim jumped up and down on the spot.

"No. I mean – jump off the bridge!"

"What?" Tim looked at me as if I was mad.

Bastille was only five steps away from us now. I ran to the edge of the bridge, hoisted myself up and jumped. Tim did the same, a few seconds behind me. I caught a glimpse of Bastille, staring at us, his face twisted between anger and amazement. Then I was falling through space with the river, the bridge and the boat corkscrewing around me. I thought I might have mistimed it but then my feet hit something and I crashed onto the deck. I was lucky. I had hit the front of the boat where there was a sheet of tarpaulin stretched out amid a tangle of ropes. It broke my fall.

Tim was less fortunate. He had jumped a few seconds after me, allowing the boat to travel a few metres further forward. I heard the glass shatter as he went feet first through the glass roof. There were more screams and the music stopped. I pulled myself up and gazed groggily through a window. Tim had landed on one of the tables and was lying there, sprawled out, surrounded by broken plates and glasses and with what looked like a whole roast duck in his lap.

"*Que fais-tu? Qu'est-ce que se passe?*"

A man in a blue uniform had appeared on the deck. He was staring at me in horror. It was the captain of the Bateau Mouche. There were a couple of waiters with him. I didn't even struggle as the three of them grabbed hold of me. I wondered if they were going to lock me up or throw me over the side. Certainly it didn't look as if they were going to invite me in for a dance and something to eat.

I twisted round and took one last look back at the bridge. Bastille and Lavache were leaning over the side, watching, and as I was dragged inside they vanished, swallowed up in the gathering gloom.

DOWN AND OUT

You won't meet many thirteen-year-olds who have been locked up in prisons on both sides of the Channel, but I'm one of them. I did time in Strangeday Hall, sharing a cell with Johnny Powers, England's public enemy number one*, and here I was in prison in Paris, this time with Tim. It was half past nine in the evening. We'd been given dinner – bread and water – but the fact that it was French bread and Perrier didn't make it taste any better.

Miraculously, neither Tim nor I had been hurt jumping from the bridge. The captain had locked us both up in the kitchen on board the ship and by the time we docked, the police were already waiting. I suppose he must have radioed on ahead. I hadn't tried to argue as we were thrown into the back of a van and driven at high speed through the streets of Paris.

* See *Public Enemy Number Two*

Nobody spoke English and even if they had they wouldn't have believed us. I assumed they'd call the British consul or someone. I would leave the explanations until then.

Neither of us had said anything for a while but at last Tim broke the silence. "That's the last time I buy a Bestlé yoghurt," he muttered.

"It wasn't their fault, Tim," I said, although I knew how he felt. We hadn't even been in Paris one day and we'd witnessed one murder, been chased by two killers and were now locked up ourselves. It was probably just as well that we weren't planning to stay a whole week. "I just wish I knew what it was all about," I added.

"They tried to kill us, Nick," Tim explained. "They nearly *did* kill us!"

"I noticed, Tim. But why?"

Tim thought for a moment. "Perhaps they don't like foreigners?" he suggested.

"No. They were looking for something. Something they thought we had." I already knew it had to be tied in with Marc Chabrol, the steward we had met at the Gare du Nord, and the sachet of sugar he had given us. But what could be so important about a packet of sugar? It was still in my back pocket. I reached in and took it out. "This is what they were after," I said.

"Sugar?"

"Unless there's something else inside..."

I was about to open it there and then but at that moment the door opened and a young policeman with close-cropped hair and glasses walked in. I slipped the sachet back into my pocket. I could always examine it later.

"This way, please," the policeman said.

He led us back out and down a corridor, then into an interrogation room that smelled of cigarette smoke. There was a table and three chairs but nothing else, not even a window. A naked light bulb hung on a short flex from the ceiling. The policeman gestured and we all sat down.

"You are English," he said.

"That's right," I said. The man obviously had a first-class brain.

"This is an outrage!" Tim exclaimed. "You can't keep us here. I demand to speak to the British ambassador! If the British ambassador is busy, I'll speak to his wife."

The policeman leaned forward. "First of all, monsieur, I can keep you here for as long as I wish," he said. "And secondly, I doubt very much that the British ambassador would be interested in you. Or his wife!"

"Why wouldn't he be interested in his wife?" Tim asked.

The policeman ignored him. "You and your small brother have caused great damage to one of our Bateaux Mouches," he went on. "It is most fortunate that nobody was injured. I wish to know why the two of you jumped off the bridge. You were trying to commit suicide, perhaps? Or could it have been a joke?"

"It was no joke," I said. "There were two men trying to kill us…"

The policeman looked at me in disbelief.

"It's true," I went on. "They said their names were Bastille and Lavache. They had a knife…"

"Tell me your names," the policeman commanded. He took out a notebook and prepared to write.

"I'm Tim Diamond," Tim said. "You may have heard of me."

"No, monsieur…"

"Well, I'm a well-known detective back in London." Tim pointed at the notebook. "That's the capital of England," he added, helpfully.

The policeman paused and took a deep breath. He was getting older by the minute. "I am aware of that," he said. "May I ask, what is your business here in Paris?"

"Of course you can ask!" Tim said.

The policeman groaned. "What is your business?" he demanded.

"We're on holiday," I told him. "We only arrived today. We're staying in Le Chat Gris in the Latin quarter…"

The policeman looked at me strangely, as if he were seeing me properly for the first time.

"Le Chat Gris…" he repeated. He closed the notebook. "Could you please wait here for a minute."

He stood up and left the room.

In fact it was ten minutes before he returned. The moment he walked in, I noticed there was something different about him. He was brisk, emotionless. And when he spoke, he did his best not to meet our eyes. "I have spoken with my superior officer," he said. "And he says that you are free to go!"

"How can we be free to go when we're locked up in here?" Tim asked.

"No, no, no, monsieur. He says that you may leave."

"They're unlocking the door and letting us out," I explained.

"As far as we are concerned, this incident is closed." The policeman did the same to his notebook.

"What about Bastille and Lavache?" I asked.

"We have no record of these men. It is our view that they do not exist!"

"What?"

"You jump off the bridge for a joke or maybe as a game and you make up the story of the killers to explain your actions. That is the view of my Superintendent."

"Well, he can't be as super as all that," I growled.

But there was no point arguing. For whatever their reasons, the French police had decided to let us go. As far as I was concerned, I just wanted to get out of jail. And out of Paris too, for that matter. I'd only been there for a day but so far our visit had been less fun than a French lesson – and twice as dangerous.

"Let's go, Tim," I said.

And we went.

It was almost eleven o'clock by the time we got back to the Latin quarter, but the night wasn't over yet. Tim wanted to stop for a beer and I was still anxious to open the packet of sugar that was burning a hole in my back pocket. We looked for a café and quite by coincidence found ourselves outside an old-fashioned, artistic sort of place whose name I knew. It was La Palette, the very same café where the train steward, Marc Chabrol, had asked us to meet.

He wasn't there, of course. Right now, if Chabrol was sipping coffee, it was with two wings and a halo. But there was someone there that we recognized. He was sitting out in the front, smoking a cigar, gazing into the night sky. There was no way I'd forget the hat. It was Jed Mathis, the businessman we had met on the train.

Tim saw him. "It's Ned," he said.

"You mean Jed," I said.

"Why don't we join him?"

"Forget it!" I grabbed Tim and we walked forward, continuing towards our hotel.

"But Nick! He paid for the drinks on the train. Maybe he'd buy me a beer."

"Yes, Tim. But think for a minute. What's he doing at La Palette?" I looked at my watch. It was eleven o'clock exactly. "It could just be a coincidence. But maybe he's waiting for someone. Maybe he's waiting for us! Don't you remember what Marc Chabrol said?"

"He asked us if we wanted to buy a KitKat."

"Yes. But after that. In the station, he warned us about someone who he called 'the mad American'. Jed Mathis is American! He said he was from Texas."

"You think Mathis killed Chabrol?"

"Mathis was on the train. And Chabrol ended up underneath it. I don't know. But I don't think we should hang around and have drinks with him. I think we should go home!"

We hurried on. Le Chat Gris loomed up ahead of us, but before we got there I noticed something else.

There was a man standing opposite the hotel. It was hard to recognize him because he was holding a camera up to his face, taking a picture. I heard the click of the button and the whir as the film wound on automatically. He wasn't a tourist. That much was certain. Not unless his idea of a holiday snap was two

English tourists about to check out. Because the photograph he had taken had been of us. There could be no doubt about it. I could feel the telephoto lens halfway up my nose.

He lowered the camera and now I recognized the man. He had been standing in the reception area that morning when we left: a dark-haired man in a grey suit.

Marc Chabrol, the steward.

Bastille and Lavache.

And now this.

Just what was happening in Paris and why did it all have to happen to us?

A car suddenly drew up, a blue Citroën. The man with the camera got in and a moment later they were roaring past us. I just caught a glimpse of the driver, smoking a cigarette with one hand, steering with the other. Then they were gone.

Tim had already walked into the hotel. Feeling increasingly uneasy, I followed him in.

We took the key from the squinting receptionist and took the stairs back to the top of the hotel. There were a lot of them and the stairway was so narrow that the walls brushed both my shoulders as I climbed. Finally we got to the last floor. Tim stopped for breath. Then he unlocked our door.

Our room had been torn apart. The sheets had been pulled off the bed and the mattress slashed open, springs and enough hair to cover a horse tumbling out onto the floor. Every drawer had been opened, upturned and smashed. The carpet had been pulled up and the curtains down. Tim's jackets and trousers had been scattered all over the room. And I mean scattered. We found one arm on a window-sill, one leg in the shower, a single pocket under what was left of the bed. Our suitcases had been cut open and turned inside out. We'd need another suitcase just to carry the old ones down to the bin.

Tim gazed at the destruction. "I can't say I think too much of room service, Nick," he said.

"This isn't room service, Tim!" I exploded. "The room's been searched!"

"What do you think they were looking for?"

"This!" I took out the packet of sugar. Once again I was tempted to open it – but this wasn't the right time. "This is the only thing Chabrol gave us back at the station. It must be the object that Bastille was talking about." I slid it back into my pocket, then thought again. It seemed that Bastille was determined to get his hands on the sugar. I wouldn't be safe carrying it. It was better to leave it in the hotel room. After all, they'd already searched the place once. It was unlikely they'd think of coming back.

I looked around, then slid the sugar into the

toilet-roll in the bathroom, inside the cardboard tube. Nobody would notice it there and the police could pick it up later. Because that was the next step.

"We've got to call the police," I said.

"We've just come from the police," Tim reminded me.

"I know. But if they see our room, they've got to believe us. And as soon as they're here, I'll show them the packet. Maybe they'll be able to work the whole thing out."

I looked for the telephone and eventually found it – or what was left of it. You'd have to be an expert at electronics or at least very good at jigsaws to use it again.

"Why don't we talk to the man downstairs?" Tim asked.

I thought of the squinting receptionist. Only that morning he'd been talking to the man in the grey suit, the one who'd just taken our photograph.

"I don't trust him," I said. At that moment I wouldn't have trusted my own mother.

Tim held up a short-sleeved shirt. It had been a long-sleeved shirt when he had packed it. He looked as if he was going to burst into tears. At least he could use the rest of the shirt as a handkerchief if he did.

"Let's go back down, Tim," I said. "We can call the police from the lobby. I noticed a phone booth."

"What's the French for 999?" Tim asked.

"17," I replied. I'd seen it written next to the phone.

But the phone in the hotel was out of order. There was a sign on the window reading *"Hors de service"*. I translated for Tim and he went over to the receptionist. "We want to call the police," he said.

"Please?" The receptionist narrowed his eye. I think he would have liked to have narrowed both his eyes, but the one on the left wasn't working.

"No," Tim explained. "Police." He saluted and bent his knees, doing an imitation of a policeman. The receptionist stared at him as if he had gone mad.

"Les flics," I said.

"Ah!" The receptionist nodded. Then he leant forward and pointed. "You go out the door. You turn left. Then you take the first turning left again," he growled. He actually spoke pretty good English even if the words had trouble getting past his throat. "There's a police station just at the next corner."

We left the hotel, turned left and then immediately left again. We found ourselves in a narrow alleyway that twisted its way through the shadows before coming to a brick wall.

"This is wrong," I said.

"You don't want to go to the police anymore?" Tim asked.

"No, Tim. I still want to go to the police but this is the wrong way. It's a dead-end."

"Maybe we have to climb over the wall."

"I don't think so..."

I was getting worried. After everything that had happened to us so far, the last place I wanted to be was a dead-end ... or anywhere else with the word "dead" in it. And I was right. There was a sudden squeal as a van appeared racing towards us. The squeal, incidentally, came from Tim. The van was reversing. For a moment I thought it was going to crush us, but it stopped, just centimetres away. The back doors flew open. Two men got out.

Everything was happening too quickly. I couldn't even tell who the men were or if I had seen them before. I saw one of them lash out and Tim spun round, crumpling to the ground. Then it was my turn. Something hard hit me on the back of the head. My legs buckled. I fell forward and one of the men must have caught me as I felt myself being half-pushed, half-carried into the back of the van.

Tim was next to me. "Some holiday!" he said.

Then either they hit me again or they hit him. Or maybe they hit both of us. Either way, I was out cold.

PARIS BY NIGHT

I knew I was in trouble before I even opened my eyes. For a start, I was sitting up. If everything that had happened up until now had been a horrible dream – which it should have been – I would be lying in my nice warm bed in Camden with the kettle whistling in the kitchen and maybe Tim doing the same in the bath. But not only was I sitting in a hard, wooden chair, my feet were tied together with something that felt suspiciously like parcel tape and my hands were similarly bound behind my back. When I did finally open my eyes, it only got worse. Tim was next to me looking pale and confused ... by which I mean even more confused than usual. And Bastille and Lavache were sitting opposite us, both of them smoking.

The four of us were in a large, empty room that might once have been the dining-room of a grand château but was now empty and dilapidated. The floor was wooden and the walls white plaster, with no pictures or decorations. A broken chandelier hung from the ceiling. In fact quite a lot of the ceiling was hanging from the ceiling. Half of it seemed to be peeling off.

I had no idea how much time had passed since they'd knocked us out and bundled us into the back of a delivery van. An hour? A week? I couldn't see my watch – it was pinned somewhere behind me, along with the wrist it was on – so I twisted round and looked out of the window. The glass was so dust-covered that I could barely see outside, but from the light I would have said it was early evening. If so, we had been unconscious for about fifteen hours! I wondered where we were. Somewhere in the distance I thought I heard singing, the sound of a choir. But the music was foreign – and not French. It sounded vaguely religious, which made me think of churches. And that made me think of funerals. I just hoped they weren't singing for us.

"Good evening," Bastille muttered. He hadn't changed out of the dirty linen suit he had been wearing when we met him the day before. It was so crumpled now that I wondered if he had slept in it.

"What time is it?" Tim asked.

"It is time for you to talk!" Bastille blew a cloud of smoke into Tim's face.

Tim coughed. "You know those things can damage your health!" he remarked.

Not quickly enough, I thought. But I said nothing.

"It is *your* health that should concern you, my friend," Bastille replied.

"I'm perfectly well, thank you," Tim said.

"I mean – your health if you fail to tell us what we want to know!" Bastille's green eyes flared. He was even uglier when he was angry. "You have put us to a great deal of trouble," he went on. "We've searched you and this morning we searched your room. Are you going to tell us where it is?"

"It's on the top floor of the hotel!" Tim exclaimed.

"Not the room!" Bastille swore and choked on his cigarette. "I am talking about the packet that you were given by Marc Chabrol."

"The ex-steward," Lavache added. He giggled, and, looking at his ape-like hands, I suddenly knew how Chabrol had managed to "fall" under a train.

I'd said nothing throughout all this. I was just glad that I'd decided not to bring the packet with us. The two men must have searched Tim and me while we were unconscious. They had found nothing and it looked like they weren't going to go back and search the hotel room a second time.

"He gave us a cup of coffee," Tim was

saying. "But we drank it. Unless you're talking about … wait a minute…"

"Who *are* you people?" I cut in. I didn't want him to say any more. So long as we had the sachet, they wouldn't kill us. They needed to know where it was. But the moment they heard it was hidden in the toilet, we were dead. That much was certain. I would just have to keep them talking and hope for the best. "Look…" I went on. "The steward didn't give us anything. We're just here on holiday."

"*Non, non, non!*" Bastille shook his head. "Do not try lying to me, *mon petit ami*. I know that your brother is a private detective. I also know that he was sent to Paris by Interpol. I know that he is working on a special assignment." His face turned ugly, which, with his face, wasn't difficult. "Now I want you to tell me how much you know and who gave you your information."

"But I don't know anything!" Tim wailed.

He'd never spoken a truer word in his life. Tim knew nothing about any special assignment. He'd have had trouble telling anyone his own shoe size. And he also hadn't realized that this was all his fault. If only he'd kept his mouth shut on the train! He'd told Jed Mathis and the old woman that he was working for Interpol. Could one of them have passed it on? Jed Mathis…?

Beware the mad American…

48

It was too late to worry about that. I realized that Tim was still talking. He had told them everything. The competition on the yoghurt pot. The free weekend. The truth.

"He's right," I admitted. "We're just tourists. We're not working for anyone."

"It was a strawberry yoghurt!" Tim burbled. "Bestlé yoghurts. They're only eighty calories each..."

"We don't know anything!" I said.

Bastille and Lavache moved closer to each other and began to mutter in low, dark voices. I couldn't understand a word they were saying, but somehow I didn't like the sound of it. I tried to break free from the chair but it was useless. Things weren't looking good. By now they must have realized that they were wrong about us, that we were exactly what we said. But they weren't just going to order us a taxi and pretend the whole thing had never happened. As they're always saying in the old movies ... we knew too much. I still had no idea who they were or what they were doing, but we knew their names and had seen their faces. That was enough.

The two men straightened up. "We have decided that we believe you," Bastille said.

"That's terrific!" Tim exclaimed.

"So now we are going to kill you."

"Oh!" His face fell.

Lavache walked to the far side of the room

and I strained my neck to watch him. He reached out with both hands and suddenly a whole section of the wall slid to one side. I realized now that it wasn't a wall at all but a set of floor-to-ceiling doors. There was another room on the other side, filled with activity, and at that moment I realized what this was all about. Perhaps I should have guessed from the start.

Drugs.

The other room was a laboratory. I could see metal tables piled high with white powder. More white powder being weighed on complicated electronic scales. White powder being spooned into plastic bags. There were about half-a-dozen people working there, young men and women with dirty faces but pristine laboratory coats. They were handling the white powder in complete silence, as if they knew that it was death they were carrying in their hands and that if it heard them it would somehow find them out.

Lavache lumbered into the room, vanishing from sight. When he reappeared, he was holding something which he handed to Bastille. Right then I was more scared than I've ever been in my life, and you know me ... I don't scare easily. But suddenly I remembered that I was thirteen years old, that I hadn't started shaving yet and that my mother (who'd been shaving for years) was thousands of miles away. I was so scared I almost wanted to cry.

Bastille was holding a bottle of pills.

He approached Tim first. "These are super-strength," he said. "I think five of them will be enough."

"No, thank you," Tim said. "I haven't got a headache."

"They're not headache pills, Tim," I said.

Bastille grabbed hold of Tim and forced his mouth open. He had counted five pills into the palm of his hand and I watched, powerless, as he forced them down Tim's throat. Then he turned and began to walk towards me.

"They don't taste very nice!" I heard Tim say, but then I'd gone crazy, rocking back and forth, yelling, kicking with my feet, trying to tear apart the parcel tape around my wrists. It was useless. I felt Lavache grab hold of my shoulders while at the same time, Bastille took hold of my chin. I don't know what was worse. Feeling his bony fingers against my face or knowing there was nothing I could do as he forced my mouth open. His right hand came up and the next moment there were four or five pills on my tongue. They had an evil taste. I drew a breath, meaning to spit them out, but his hand was already over my mouth, almost suffocating me. I screamed silently and felt the pills trickle down the back of my throat. I almost felt them drop into the pit of my stomach. Then Bastille pulled his hand clear and my head sank forward. I said nothing. I thought I was dead. I thought he had killed me.

Things happened very quickly after that. It seemed to me that the lights in the room had brightened and that somebody had turned up the heating. My eyes were hurting. And then the walls began to revolve, slowly at first, like the start of a ride at a funfair. But there was nothing fun about this. Drugs are poison and I was sure I had just been given a lethal overdose. I was sweating. I tried to speak but my tongue refused to move; anyway, my mouth was too dry.

I heard the parcel tape being ripped off and felt my hands come free. Lavache was standing behind me. I tried to look at him, but my head lolled uselessly. He pulled me off the chair and carried me outside. Bastille followed with Tim.

There was a white van waiting for us in an enclosed courtyard – we could have been anywhere. I looked back at the house we had just left. It was a grey building, three storeys high. Most of its paint had flaked off and there were scorch marks, as if it had been involved in a fire. About half the windows were shattered. Others had been bricked in. The place looked derelict. I guessed it was supposed to.

I was bundled into the van and the next moment the engine started up, roaring at me like a mechanical beast. I almost expected it to come bursting through the floor, to gobble me up. The noise hammered at my ears and I groaned. Tim was thrown in next to me. The doors slammed. My stomach heaved. We were off.

There was a small window set in the door and I managed to stagger over to it and pull myself onto my knees to look out. But it was hard to see anything. The world was spinning faster now, tilting from side to side. I just made out a series of letters in red neon, but it seemed to take me for ever to work out the three words they formed:

THE FRENCH CONFECTION

The van turned a corner and I lost my balance. Before I fell, I caught a glimpse of a blue star … on a flag or perhaps on the side of a building. Then the sound of the van's engine rose up again and swallowed me. The floor hit me in the face. Or maybe it was me who had hit the floor. I no longer knew the difference.

The journey took an hour … a month … a year. I no longer had any idea. What was the stuff they had given me? Whatever it was, it was taking over, killing me. I could feel it happening, an inch at a time. The van stopped. Hands that no longer belonged to bodies pulled us out. Then the pavement slapped me in the face, there was another scream from the engine and suddenly I knew that we were alone.

"Tim...?" I gasped the word. But Tim was no longer there. He had turned into some horrible animal with sixteen eyes, tentacles and...

I forced myself to concentrate, knowing that it was the drug that was doing it to me. The image dissolved and there he was again. My brother.

"Nick..." He staggered to his feet. All three of them. Things weren't back to normal yet.

The sky changed from red to blue to yellow to green. I stood up as well.

"Must get help," I said.

Tim groaned.

We were back in the centre of Paris. It was late at night. And Paris had never looked like this before.

There was the Seine but the water had gone, replaced by red wine that glowed darkly in the moonlight. It was twisting its way underneath the bridges, but now that I looked more closely, I saw that they had changed too. They had become huge sticks of French bread. There was a sudden buzzing. A Bateau Mouche had suddenly sprouted huge blue wings and legs. It leapt out of the water and onto one of the bridges, tearing a great chunk out with a hideous, hairy mouth before spiralling away into the night.

The ground underneath my feet had gone

soft and I realized I was sinking into it. With a cry I lifted one foot and saw that the tar had melted and was dripping off my trainer. Except the tar was yellow, not black.

"It's cheese!" I shouted. And it was. The entire street had turned into cheese – soft, ripe, French cheese. I gasped for air, choking on the smell. At the same time, the cheese pulled me into it. Another few seconds and I would be sucked underneath the surface.

"Nick!" Tim called out.

And then the cheese was gone as he pointed with an arm that was now a mile long. There was a snail coming down the Boulevard. No … not one snail but a thousand of them, each one the size of a house, slithering along ahead of the traffic, leaving a grey, slimy trail behind them. At one corner, the traffic lights had gone red and all the snails were squeaking at each other, a fantastic traffic jam of snails. At the same time, I heard what sounded like a gigantic burp and a frog, the size of a bus, bounded across my vision, leaping over a building. But the frog was missing its legs. It was supporting itself on giant crutches.

The world twisted, heaved, broke up and then reformed with all the pieces in different positions: a jigsaw in the hands of a destructive child.

Suddenly we were surrounded by grinning stone figures, jabbering and staring at us with empty stone eyes. I recognized them: the gargoyles from Notre Dame. There must have been a hundred of them. One of them was sitting on Tim's shoulder like a grey chimpanzee. But Tim didn't seem to have noticed it.

Light. Car lights. Everywhere. A horn sounded. I had stepped into the road – but it didn't matter because the cars were the size of matchboxes. They were all Citroëns. Every one of them. And they were being followed by cyclists. The Tour de France had come early that year. All the cyclists were smoking cigarettes.

Tim was clutching a streetlamp. Now he was wearing a striped jersey and a beret and there was a string of onions hanging from his side. "*Je suis,*" he said. "*Tu es, il est...*"

I opened my mouth to reply.

Crash! Crash! Crash!

I saw it before he did. Perhaps he didn't see it at all. Even now, with the drug pumping through my body, I knew that it wasn't real, that I was hallucinating. But it made no difference. As far as I was concerned, everything I saw was real. And if it was real, it could kill me. It could step on me. It could crush me.

The Eiffel Tower! On our first day in Paris we had crossed the city to visit it. Now the Eiffel Tower was coming to visit us. There it was, walking across Paris, swinging one iron foot, then the next, moving like some sort of giant, four-legged crab. One of its feet came down in a pancake stall. Wood shattered. Pancakes flew in all directions. Somebody screamed.

The cheese was getting softer. I was sinking into a boulevard of Brie, a dual carriageway of Camembert. The squirming yellow slipped round my waist, rose over my shoulder and twisted round my neck. I didn't even try to fight. I'd had enough. I waited for it to pull me under.

I thought I was going to die and if I'd waited another minute I might well have. But just then I heard what I thought was an owl, hooting in my ear. At the same time, I found myself staring at a face I knew. A dark-haired man in a grey-coloured suit. I became aware of a blue flashing light which either belonged to a dragon or a police car. I looked up and saw something driving out of the moon, flying through the sky towards me. An ambulance.

"Don't go to sleep!" a voice commanded. "Don't go to sleep! Don't go to sleep!"

But it was too late. I went to sleep.

For ever.

THE MAD AMERICAN

"You're lucky to be alive," the man said.

It was two days later. I don't want to tell you about those two days. I'd spent both of them in hospital in Paris and all I can say is, if you've ever had your stomach pumped, you'll know there are plenty of things you can do that are more fun. I don't remember much about the first day. The next day, I felt like a spin-drier that's been left on too long. All I'd eaten in the entire time was a little bread and water. Fortunately, the water didn't have bubbles. I don't think I could have managed the bubbles.

And now, here I was in the headquarters of Sûreté, the French police force. It's funny how police stations are the same the whole world over. This may have been grander and smarter than New Scotland Yard. The curtains were velvet and the pictures on the wall showed some grey-haired Frenchman in a suit rather than our own grey-haired Queen in a crown. But it still smelled the same.

Tim was sitting next to me. He was the colour of the yoghurt that had brought us here in the first place, with eyes like crushed strawberries. His hair was dishevelled and he looked like he hadn't slept in a month. I was going to say something but decided against it. I probably looked just as bad.

We were in the office of the Chief of Police – a man called Christien Moire. I knew because I'd seen the name and title on the door. It was on his desk too. Maybe he was worried he was going to forget it. He was the man in the grey suit whom I'd seen standing outside Le Chat Gris, the man who had been talking to the receptionist and who had later taken our photograph. Things were beginning to add up even if I still had no idea of the sum total.

"Another one hour and it would have been too late," Moire went on. He spoke English as if he had no idea what he was saying, lingering on every word. He had the sort of accent you get in bad television plays: *Anuzzer wan our an' eet would 'ave bin too late.* I hope you get the idea. "You were very lucky," he added.

"Sure," I muttered. "And we'd have been even luckier if you'd arrived a couple of hours before."

Moire shrugged. "I'm sorry," he said. But

his dark, empty eyes looked about as apologetic as two lumps of ice. "We had no idea you had been taken," he went on.

"Who are you?" Tim demanded. "You call yourself the Sûreté. But what exactly are you sure about?"

"The Sûreté," Moire repeated, "is the French police force. I am the head of a special unit fighting the traffic in …"

"…drugs." I completed the sentence.

"*Exactement*. I have to say that you and your brother seem to have turned up in the wrong place at the wrong time. If I hadn't been watching you…"

"You were at the hotel," I said. "I saw you outside. You had a camera…"

"Is that your hobby?" Tim asked. "Photography?"

Christien Moire stared at Tim through narrow eyes. He obviously hadn't ever met anyone like him before. "Le Chat Gris has been under surveillance," he said. "Perhaps I should explain…"

"Perhaps you should," I said.

Moire lit a Gauloise. It's a funny thing about the French. Not only do they all smoke, but they smoke the most horrible cigarettes in the world. Forget about the health warning on the packet. The smoke from Moire's cigarette was so thick, you could have printed it on that.

"For some time now," he began, "we have

been aware of a drug-smuggling operation. Somebody has been moving drugs to London ... using the trains under the channel. We still don't know how they're doing it. We have searched the trains from top to bottom but we have found nothing. Worse still, we do not know who they are."

"Is there anything you *do* know?" I asked.

Moire glanced at me with unfriendly eyes. "We know only the code-name of the man behind the operation," he replied.

"The Mad American," I said.

That surprised Moire, but he tried not to show it. "The drugs arrive from Marseilles," he went on. "They are weighed and packaged somewhere in Paris. Then the Mad American arranges for them to be sent to London. We've been working with the English police to try to stop them. So far we have had no success in London. But in Paris we had one lucky break."

"Le Chat Gris," I said.

"Yes, we learned that the hotel is sometimes used by the Mad American. When dealers arrive from London to buy his drugs, that is where they stay. He meets them there. They pay him the money and then his two associates – Jacques Bastille and Luc Lavache – arrange for the drugs to be sent on the train."

"So *that's* why you photographed us!" I said. "You thought we'd come to Paris to buy drugs!"

"I know it sounds unlikely," Moire said. "An English kid and his idiotic brother –"

"Nick isn't idiotic!" Tim protested.

"We became interested in you the moment you reported that Bastille and Lavache had attempted to kill you," Moire went on. "I ordered the photograph to be taken so that we could check you against our criminal files."

"But if you thought we were criminals, why did you let us go in the first place?" I asked. It had puzzled me at the time, the policeman suddenly changing his mind and telling us we could leave.

"The answer to that is simple," Moire said. "We still had no idea what part you had to play in all this, but you had mentioned Le Chat Gris and that was enough. It was important that the Mad American should not be aware that the police were involved. I personally ordered your release, and at the same time I made sure that we kept you under – how do you say? – surveillance. This was very lucky for you, considering how things turned out."

"You were following us."

"Yes. I saw you go back to the hotel, and minutes later I saw the van with the two men who knocked you out and kidnapped you. We followed the van but unfortunately lost it in traffic..."

"...so you don't know where we were taken."

"No. But I knew that you were in danger and I had every gendarme in Paris looking out for you. One of them saw you and radioed HQ. By that time they had pumped you with enough drugs to kill a horse."

"Why would they want to kill a horse?" Tim asked.

Moire ignored him. "We only got to you in the nick of time. Another ten minutes, and the two of you would now be in Père Lachaise."

"You mean, another hotel," Tim said.

"No. Père Lachaise is a cemetery."

"OK. You saved us, Monsieur Moire," I said. "But now, if you don't mind, I'm heading back to the hotel, packing and leaving for London."

"That's right, Monsieur Loire," Tim agreed. "We're out of here!"

"I'm afraid not." Moire hadn't raised his voice. If anything, he had done the exact opposite. But that's the thing about the French. When they're being really nasty, they don't shout. They whisper. "You realize that I could have you arrested?" he asked.

I almost laughed. "What for?" I demanded.

"You were found in the middle of Paris, full of drugs," the police chief explained. He sounded almost reasonable. "Two English tourists who decided to experiment with these forbidden substances…"

"That's a complete lie!" I exclaimed.

"Yes!" Tim agreed. "We're not tourists!"

"And then there is the matter of the Bateau Mouche..." Moire continued. "You jumped off a bridge, endangering the lives of the people on the boat. This could also prove to be drug-related."

"What do you want, Moire?" I demanded.

Moire leaned forward. His face could have been carved out of stone. Even the cigarette smoke seemed to have solidified. "There are two things we wish to find out," he said. "First, who is the Mad American?"

"Why don't you ask Bastille and Lavache?" I demanded.

"They wouldn't tell us anything. And if we did arrest them, it would only let their boss know that we were getting close ... and that would ruin everything. The second thing we wish to know is, how are they smuggling the drugs across the Channel? As I have told you, we have searched the train many times ... but with no success. These packets of white powder – they must be somewhere. But..." He smacked his forehead with the palm of his hand. "It is infuriating!"

"What do you want us to do?" I asked.

"I want you to go back to the hotel," Moire replied. "It will be as if nothing has happened."

"Why?"

"Because you can be useful to me ... on the

inside. My men will continue to watch you. You'll be completely safe. But maybe you can find the answers to the questions. And if there is anything to report…"

"Forget it!" I snapped.

"Right!" Tim nodded. "Bestlé only paid for four days. We can't possibly afford it."

"Bestlé?" For the first time Moire looked puzzled. "Who is Bestlé?"

"It doesn't matter," I replied. "We're British citizens. You can't blackmail us!"

"You don't think so?" Moire almost smiled. "You are Europeans now, my friend. And if you don't do exactly as I tell you, let me assure you that you will be spending a great deal of time inside a European jail."

I wanted to argue, but I could see there was no point. The last person to argue with Christien Moire probably found himself with a one-way ticket to Devil's Island.

He knew he'd beaten me. "Go back to Le Chat Gris and wait for further instructions," he said. "Don't worry about the bill. I will see to it."

"And what if we get killed?" I asked.

"My department will pay for the funeral too."

I sank back in my chair. There was nothing I could say. Not in French. Not in English. It really wasn't fair.

* * *

And that was how we found ourselves, a few hours later, back in our room at Le Chat Gris. As I'd walked back into the hotel, I'd known how those French aristocrats must have felt as they took their last steps towards the guillotine. The receptionist had almost fallen off his chair when he saw us and he'd been on the telephone before we'd reached the lift. The Mad American would have presumed we were dead. Now he'd know he was wrong. How long would it take him to correct his mistake?

Tim sat down on the bed. He was actually looking quite cheerful, which made me feel even worse. "Maybe this isn't so bad, Nick," he said.

"Tim!" I cried. "How bad can it get?"

"We're working for the French police now," he said. "This could be good for business! *Tim Diamond Inc ... London and Paris*. That'll look good on the door."

"It'll look even better on your gravestone," I said. "Don't you understand, Tim?" We're not working for anyone! Christien Moire was lying through his teeth!"

"You mean ... he isn't a policeman?"

"Of course he's a policeman. But he doesn't want us to work for him. He's using us!" I'd taken a guidebook of Paris out of my case. Now I sat down next to Tim. "Moire wants to find out the identity of the Mad American," I explained. "What's the best way to do that?"

"Just ask for Tim Diamond…"

"Just *use* Tim Diamond. He's sent us back here because he knows that our turning up again will panic the Mad American. He's already tried to kill us twice. He's certain to try again – and this time Moire will be watching. He's using us as bait in a trap, Tim. The Mad American kills us. Moire gets the Mad American. It's as simple as that."

I opened the guidebook. "I'm not sitting here, waiting to be shot," I said.

"Where do you want to be shot?" Tim asked.

"I don't want to be shot anywhere! That's why I'm going to find the Mad American before he finds us." I started to thumb through the pages. I still didn't know what I was looking for, but I had a good idea. "After we were knocked out, we were taken to the Mad American's headquarters," I said.

"But we were knocked out!" Tim said. "We didn't see anything."

"We didn't see much," I agreed. "But there were some clues. A blue star. Some words in a shop window – THE FRENCH CONFECTION. And when we were tied up, I heard something. Music. Singing."

"Do you think that was the Mad American?"

"No, Tim. It was coming from a building nearby." I stopped, trying to remember what I had heard. "It wasn't French singing," I said. "It was different… It was foreign."

Sitting next to me on the bed, Tim was making a strange noise. I thought for a moment that he had stomach-ache. Then I realized he was trying to hum the tune.

"That's right, Tim," I said. "It was something like that. Only a bit more human."

Tim stopped. I tried to think. How had the singing gone? It had been sad and somehow dislocated. A choir and a single male voice. At times it had been more like wailing than singing. Remembering it now made me think of a church. Was that it? Had it been religious music? But if so, what religion?

I'm not sure what happened first. The thought seemed to come into my mind at exactly the same moment as I found myself looking at the words *The Jewish Quarter* in the guidebook in my hands.

"Jewish music!" I exclaimed.

"Jewish?"

"The music that we heard, Tim. It was coming from a synagogue!"

Tim's eyes lit up. "You think we were taken to Jerusalem?"

"No, Tim. We were in Paris. But there's an area of Paris that's full of synagogues." I waved the book at him. "Le Marais. That's what it's called. The Jewish sector of Paris…"

"But how big is it?" Tim asked.

I read the page in front of me:

Originally a swamp, the Marais has grown to become
one of the most fashionable areas of Paris. Its narrow
streets are filled with shops and boutiques including
some of the city's most elegant cafés and cake shops.
The Marais is home to the Jewish quarter with numerous synagogues and kosher restaurants based around
the Rue des Rosiers.

There was a map showing the area. It only had
a couple of dozen roads. "It doesn't look too
big," I said. "And at least we know what we're
looking for. The French Confection."

"But what *is* The French Confection,
Nick?"

"I think it must be a shop. Maybe it sells
cakes or sweets or something. But once we've
found it, we'll know we're right next to the
factory. Find the sign and we'll have found the
Mad American."

"And then?"

"Then we call Moire."

We slipped out of Le Chat Gris down the fire
escape, dodging past Moire's men who were
waiting for us at the front of the hotel. Then
we dived into the nearest Metro station and
headed north.

It was a short walk from the station to the
start of Le Marais – the Place Vendôme, one

of those Paris squares where even the trees manage to look expensive. From there we headed down towards a big, elegant building that turned out to be the Picasso museum. I'd studied Picasso at school. He's the guy who painted women with eyes in the sides of their necks and tables with legs going the wrong way. It's called surrealism. Maybe I should have taken Tim in, as he's pretty surreal himself. But we didn't have time.

We backtracked and found ourselves in a series of long, narrow streets with buildings rising five storeys on both sides. But I knew we were on the right track. There was no singing, but here and there I saw blue stars – the same stars I had glimpsed as I was bundled into the van. I knew what it was now: the six-pointed Star of David. There was one in every kosher food store and restaurant in the area.

We'd been following the Rue des Rosiers – the one I'd read about in the guidebook – but with no sign of the building where we'd been held. So now we started snaking up and down, taking the first on the right and the next on the left and so on. It was a pretty enough part of Paris, I'll say that for it. Tim had even forgotten our mission and stopped once or twice to take photographs. We'd been chased and threatened at knife-point. We'd been kidnapped, drugged and threatened again – this time by the French police. And he *still* thought we were on holiday!

And then, suddenly, we were there.

It was on one of the main streets of the area – the Rue de Sevigny. I recognized it at once: the burnt face of the building, the broken windows, the ugly chimney stacks... And there was the archway that we had driven through. There was a courtyard on the other side which was where the white van had been parked. I stood there in the sunlight, with people strolling past on the pavements, some carrying shopping bags, others pushing prams. And none of them knew. The biggest drug factory in Paris was right in front of them, just sitting there between a café and a cake shop, right in the middle of the Marais. I couldn't believe I had found it so easily. It was hard to believe it was there at all.

"Nick...!" Tim whispered.

I grabbed hold of him and pulled him down behind a parked car as Bastille and Lavache appeared, coming out of the front door and walking across the courtyard. Each of them had a heavy box in their hands. Another shipment on its way out! It made me angry that anyone should be dumb enough to want to buy drugs and angrier still that these two grim reapers would be getting richer by selling them.

"What do we do now?" Tim whispered.

"Now we call Moire," I said.

"Right!" Tim straightened up. "Let's ask in there!"

Before I could stop him he had walked across the pavement and into the cake shop. There was the sign in the window that I had seen from the van. THE FRENCH CONFECTION. Why did the name bother me? Why did I feel it was connected with something or someone I had seen? It was too late to worry about it now. Tim was already inside. I followed him in.

I found myself in a long, narrow shop with a counter running down one wall. Everywhere I looked there were cakes and croissants, bowls of coloured almonds and tiny pots of jam. The very air smelt of sugar and flour. On the counter stood one of the tallest wedding cakes I had ever seen: six platforms of swirly white icing with a marzipan bride and groom looking air-sick up on the top. There was a bead curtain at the back and now it rattled as the owner of the shop passed through, coming out to serve us. And of course I knew her. I'd met her on the train.

Erica Nice.

She stopped behind the counter, obviously as surprised to see us as we were to see her.

"You...!" she began.

"Mrs Nice!" Tim gurgled. I wondered how he had managed to remember her name. "We need to use your telephone. To call the police."

"I don't think so, Tim," I said.

Even as I spoke I was heading back towards the door. But I was already too late. Erica's hand came up and this time it wasn't holding an almond slice. It was the biggest gun I'd ever seen. Bigger than the wrinkled hand that held it. Its muzzle was as ugly as the smile on the old woman's face.

"But ... but ... but..." Tim stared.

"Erica Nice," I said. "I suppose I should have guessed. Madame Erica Nice. Say it fast and what do you get?"

"Madamericanice?" Tim suggested.

"Mad American," I said. "She's the one behind the drug racket, Tim. When we met her, she must have been checking the route. That's why she was on the train. And that's how Bastille and Lavache knew we were in Paris."

Erica Nice snarled at us. "Yes," she said. "I have to travel on the train now and then to keep an eye on things. Like that idiot steward – Marc Chabrol. He was scared. And scared people are no use to me."

"So you pushed him under a train," I said.

She shrugged. "I would have preferred to stab him. I did have my knitting needles, but unfortunately I was halfway through a woollen jumper. Pushing was easier."

"And what now?" I asked. I wondered if she was going to shoot us herself or call her two thugs to finish the job for her. At the same time,

I took a step forward, edging my way towards the counter and the giant wedding cake.

"Those idiots – Jacques and Luc – should have got rid of you when they had the chance," Erica hissed. "This time they will make no mistakes."

She turned to press a switch set in the wall. Presumably it connected the shop with the factory next door.

I leapt forward and threw my entire weight against the cake.

Erica half turned. The gun came up.

The door of the shop burst open, the glass smashing.

And as Erica Nice gave a single shrill scream and disappeared beneath about ten kilograms of wedding cake, Christien Moire and a dozen gendarmes hurled themselves into the shop. At the same time, I heard the blare of sirens as police cars swerved into the road from all directions.

I turned to Moire. "You followed us here?"

Moire nodded. "Of course. I had men on all sides of the hotel."

Erica Nice groaned and tried to fight her way out of several layers of sponge, jam and butter cream. Tim leaned forward and scooped up a fragment of white icing. He popped it into his mouth.

"Nice cake," he said.

THE WHITE CLIFFS

The next day, Christien Moire drove us up to Calais and personally escorted us onto the ferry. It would have been easier to have taken the train, of course. But somehow Tim and I had had enough of trains.

It had been a good week for Moire. Jacques Bastille and Luc Lavache had both been arrested. So had Erica Nice. The drug factory had been closed down and more arrests were expected. No wonder Moire wanted us out of the way. He was looking forward to promotion and maybe the Croix de Guerre or whatever medal French heroes get pinned to their right nipple. The last thing Moire needed was Tim and me hanging around to tell people the part we had played.

Moire stopped at the quay and handed us our tickets as well as a packed lunch for the crossing. "France is in your debt," he said, solemnly, and before either of us could stop him he had grabbed hold of Tim and planted a kiss on both cheeks.

Tim went bright red. "I know I cracked the case," he muttered. "But let's not get *too* friendly..."

"It's just the French way," I said. Even so, I made sure I shook hands with Moire. I didn't want him getting too close.

"I wish you a good journey, my friends," Moire said. "And this time, perhaps you will be careful what you say while you are on the ship!"

"We won't be saying anything," I promised. I'd bought Tim a Tintin book at the harbour bookstall. He could read that on the way home.

Moire smiled. *"Au revoir,"* he said.

"Where?" Tim asked. I'd have to translate it for him later.

We were about halfway home, this time chopping up and down on the Channel, when Tim suddenly looked up from the Tintin book. "You know," he said. "We never did find out how Erica Nice was smuggling the drugs on the train."

"Haven't you guessed?" I sighed and pulled out the blue sugar sachet that had started the whole thing. It was the sachet Tim had been given at the Gare du Nord. Somehow I'd never quite got round to opening it. I did so now.

There was a spoonful of white powder inside.

"Sugar?" Tim muttered.

"I don't think so, Tim," I replied. "This is just one sachet. But Erica Nice was transporting thousands of them every day on the train. A little parcel of drugs. One dose, already weighed and perfectly concealed." I tore open the packet and held it up. The powder was caught in the wind and snatched away. I watched it go, a brief flurry of white as it skimmed over the handrail and disappeared into the grey water of the English Channel.

"Do you think we ought to tell Moire?" Tim asked.

"I expect he's worked it out for himself," I said.

In the distance I could see the white cliffs of Dover looming up. We had only been away for a week but somehow it seemed a lot longer. I was glad to be home.

Tim was still holding the packed lunch that Moire had given us. Now he opened it. The first thing he took out was a strawberry yoghurt.

"Very funny," I said.

The yoghurt followed the drugs into the channel. Then we went downstairs to order fish and chips.

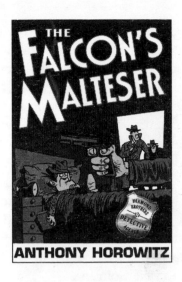

"Johnny Naples opened his mouth and tried to speak. 'The falcon...' he said. Then a nasty, bubbling sound..."

When vertically challenged Johnny Naples entrusts Tim Diamond with a package worth over three million pounds, he's making a big mistake. For Tim Diamond is probably the worst detective in the entire world. Next day, Johnny's dead. Tim gets the blame, his smart, wisecracking younger brother Nick gets the package – and every crook in town is out to get them!

"Any child with a quick sense of humour should love it... An abundance of jokes, most of them first-class."

The Times Literary Supplement

ANTHONY HOROWITZ is one of the most popular and prolific children's writers working today. His phenomenally successful Alex Rider series, comprising *Stormbreaker*, *Point Blanc*, *Skeleton Key*, *Eagle Strike*, *Scorpia* and *Ark Angel*, has sold over ten million copies worldwide and won numerous awards, including the Children's Book of the Year Award for *Ark Angel* at the 2006 British Book Awards and the Red House Children's Book Award for *Skeleton Key* in 2003. *Stormbreaker*, the first Alex Rider mission, was recently made into a blockbuster movie starring Alex Pettyfer as the teenage superspy and also Ewan McGregor, Bill Nighy and Robbie Coltrane.

Anthony's other titles for Walker Books include the hugely popular Diamond Brothers mysteries; *Groosham Grange* and its sequel, *Return to Groosham Grange*; *The Devil and His Boy*; *The Switch*; *Granny*; and The Power of Five, a series of supernatural thrillers beginning with *Raven's Gate*, *Evil Star* and *Nightrise*.

Anthony also writes extensively for TV, with credits including *Midsomer Murders*, *Poirot* and the drama series *Foyle's War*, which won the Lew Grade Audience Award in 2003. He is married to television producer Jill Green and lives in London with his two sons, Nicholas and Cassian, and their dog, Unlucky.